Louie the Tui
Learns to Sing

**Written by Janet Martin
and illustrated by Ivar Treskon**

First published in 2002 by Jampot Productions
P O Box 60593, Titirangi, Waitakere City, Auckland, New Zealand

Tui

Tuis are well known New Zealand native birds, easily recognised by their distinctive
white tufts of feathers on either side of the neck (called 'pois').

They are loved for their song, which ranges from a series of clucking, wheezing and chuckling,
to loud, rich melodious notes, and they often mimic other birds.

Tuis are honeyeaters, one of their favourite foods being the nectar from the
yellow flower of the native kowhai tree.

ISBN 0-473-08856-8

Louie the Tui from green Woodlands Park

Wanted to sing but he couldn't quite start.

Try as he might he could only just croak

While the other birds laughed
and thought Louie a joke.

Louie sat high in the tall kauri tree,

Looking around at the things he could see.

He listened with envy to other birds sing,

And tucked his head sadly under his wing.

"Why?" Louie said with an unhappy sigh

"Can't I sing just like them?" as he started to fly.

"It doesn't seem fair that a bird such as me

Must always sit silent on top of the tree."

Now Annie the Granny lived all alone

With only her cat and her red telephone,

In her house by a kauri and bright kowhai tree

All surrounded by birds
who were happy and free.

Early each morning she opened the door

And took out some bread for the birds,
and then more.

The cat was too lazy to bother the birds,

Very well fed and too pampered for words.

Louie watched Annie while Annie looked back.

"Come here little tui, and have a nice snack."

But Louie was scared of Miss Fluffy the cat,

So he stayed on the kowhai tree branch,
where he sat.

Later that day Annie sat on the deck

And played her guitar, (while Miss Fluffy just slept).

She played such a beautiful sweet melody

Louie thought "Hey! She's playing that song
just for me."

Louie was happy, he opened his beak

And out came a note
sounding just like a squeak.

Astounded, he opened his beak wider still,

Then deep from his throat Louie started to trill.

The notes just got louder, then tuneful
and clear.

He sang with a joy that was awesome to hear.

Miss Fluffy and Annie were happy and glad

That Louie was no longer downcast and sad.

Now every time Annie plays a sweet song

Louie the Tui will sing right along,

And all of the children who live near and far

Come to hear Louie, and Annie's guitar.

So next time you pass by a tall kauri tree

And hear a proud tui, singing so free,

Keep a lookout for Annie, who with her guitar

Turned a sad little Louie into a star.

The End

*For mum, who fed her bird friends every day,
and for all the grandchildren, especially Thomas, Cameron, Daniel, Jack,
Lucie, Kirralee, Zach, Ryan and Eva.*

Janet

*To Marigold, thanks for your inspiration for these drawings,
and to Mum, Dad and Justine.*

Ivar